DANNY McGEE
DRINKS THE SEA

ANDY STANTON & NEAL LAYTON

schwartz & wade books · new york

Visit us on the Web! randomhousekids.com
Educators and librarians, for a variety of teaching tools, visit us at RHTeachersLibrarians.com

Library of Congress Cataloging-in-Publication Data
Names: Stanton, Andy. | Layton, Neal, illustrator.
Title: Danny McGee drinks the sea / by Andy Stanton ; illustrated by Neal Layton.
Description: First American edition. | New York : Schwartz & Wade Books, 2017.
Originally published by Hodder Children's Books, London, in 2016.
Summary: When Danny's sister doubts his boast that he can drink the
entire sea, he not only proves he was right, he swallows everything else in sight.
Identifiers: LCCN 2016025799 (print) | LCCN 2016053902 (ebook)
ISBN 978-1-5247-1736-0 (hardback) | ISBN 978-1-5247-1737-7 (glb)
ISBN 978-1-5247-1738-4 (ebook) | ISBN 978-1-5247-1738-4 (ebk)
Subjects: | CYAC: Stories in rhyme. | Brothers and sisters—Fiction.
Humorous stories. | Tall tales. | BISAC: JUVENILE FICTION / Humorous
Stories. | JUVENILE FICTION / Family / Siblings.
Classification: LCC PZ8.3.S7879 Dan 2017 (print) | LCC PZ8.3.S7879 (ebook) | DDC [E]—dc23

The text of this book is set in StampGothic.
The illustrations were rendered in mixed media.

MANUFACTURED IN CHINA
2 4 6 8 10 9 7 5 3 1
First American Edition

Random House Children's Books supports the First Amendment and celebrates the right to read.

One summer's day, Danny
and Frannie McGee
hopped into a car
and drove down
to the sea.

The sea was all sparkly,
blue as can be.

"I bet I can drink it,"
said Danny McGee.

Said Frannie, "No, Danny,
I cannot agree.
You'll **never** drink all of it,
Danny McGee."

"I will, just you watch,"
replied Danny McGee.
"Please fetch me a straw
and then you will see."

So Fran fetched a straw that was longer than she.

And Danny McGee started drinking the sea.

In ten minutes' time
there was no sea to see,

because all of the sea
was in Danny McGee.

"I cannot believe it," said Frannie McGee. "You've drunk the whole thing.

It's **AMAZING** to me!"

"I'm **just getting started**," said Danny McGee.

And he flicked out his tongue and he swallowed a **tree**.

And he swallowed a **bird**

and he swallowed a **bee.**

And he swallowed a **cat**
who was drinking some tea.

And he swallowed a fly

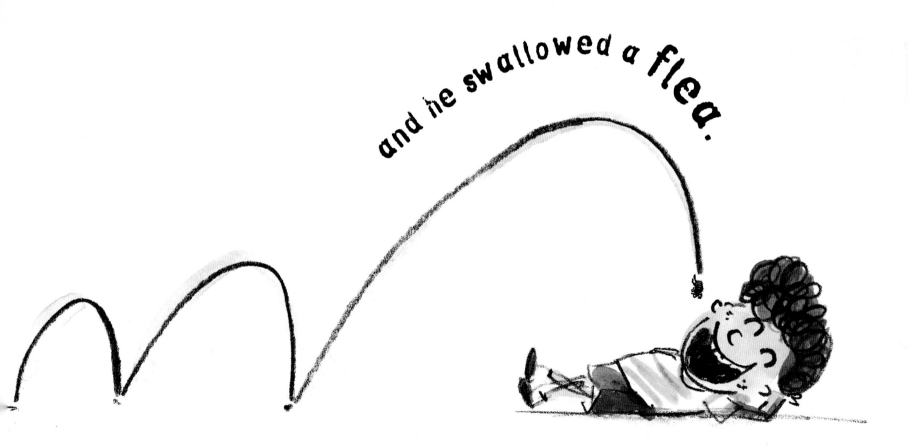

and he swallowed a flea.

And he swallowed a **man** who was learning to ski.

And he swallowed a **pie**

and he swallowed a **pea**.

And he swallowed the weather girl on the **TV**.

"You're naughty!" said Frannie.
"I'm telling, you'll see!"
But Danny just giggled . . .

and swallowed a **SWEE.**

And I know that you think there's
no such thing as a swee,
but believe me, there **was,**
before Danny McGee.

S is for "Swee"

The Swee is a hairy sort of fellow native the upper lower easter regions of the Wester Northlands of the South. Little is known about these remarkable a except that th

"I will swallow it all!" shouted Danny McGee.

And he swallowed the sand where the sea used to be.

And he swallowed the **mountains,**

and every last **tree.**

And he swallowed the **jungles**.

He did it with **glee**.

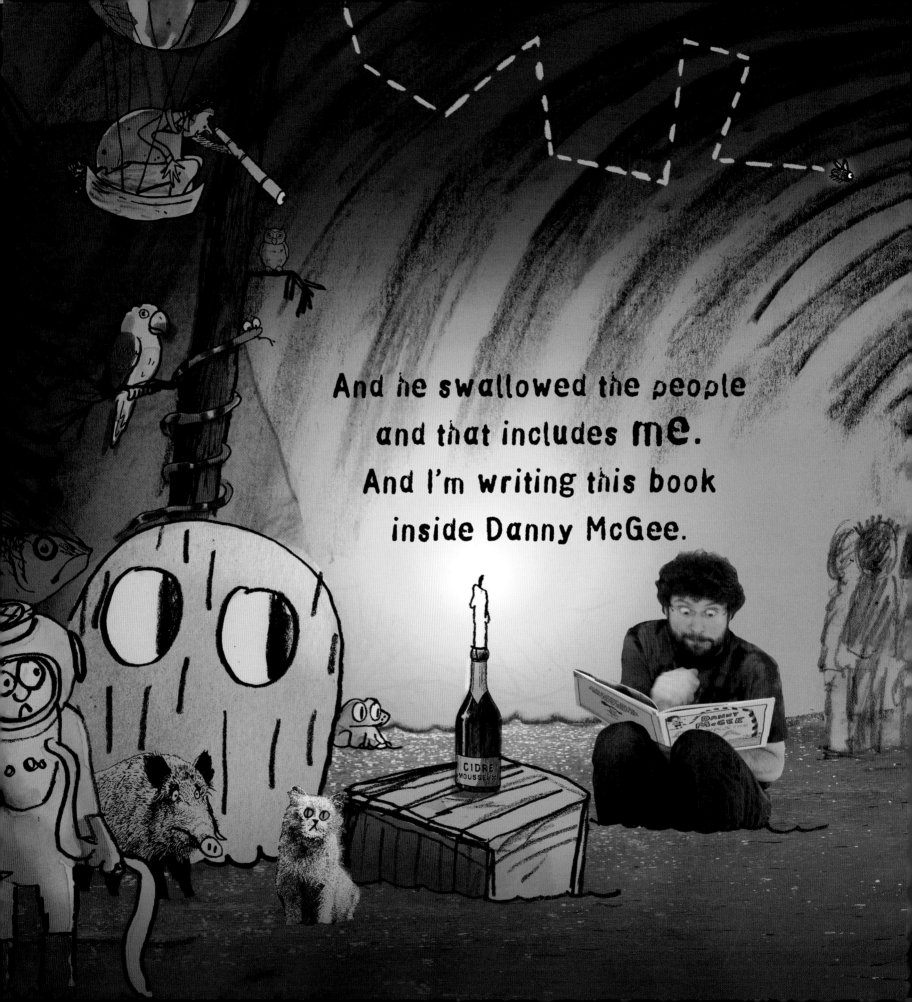

And he swallowed the people
and that includes **me**.
And I'm writing this book
inside Danny McGee.

And he swallowed America,
land of the free.

And he swallowed up London,
chim chim cher-ee!

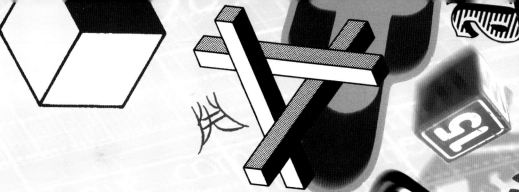

And he swallowed the alphabet  A, B, and C.

And he swallowed the numbers 1, 2, and 3.

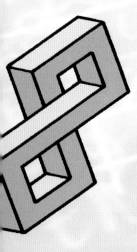

And he swallowed until
there was no more to see.

"Danny, you didn't get me."

And she opened her mouth
and s w a l l o w e d

Danny McGee.

"Little brothers can be **SO** annoying sometimes."